Lazy Lion

First published in 1990 by Hodder Children's Books
This paperback edition published in 2005

Text copyright © Bruce Hobson 1990
Illustrations copyright © Adrienne Kennaway 1990
www.brucehobson.net

Hodder Children's Books, 338 Euston Road, London, NW1 3BH

Hodder Children's Books Australia
Level 17/207 Kent Street, Sydney, NSW 2000

ISBN 978 0 340 56565 0

Printed in China

Hodder Children's Books is a division of Hachette Children's Books.
An Hachette UK Company.
www.hachette.co.uk

Lazy Lion

By
Mwenye Hadithi

Illustrated by
Adrienne Kennaway

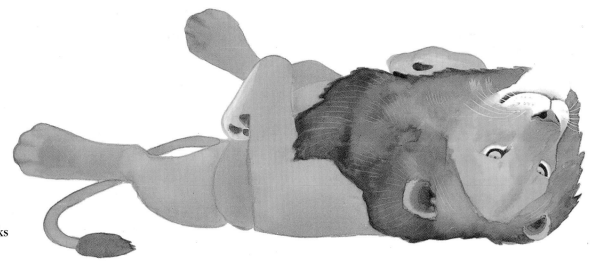

Hodder
Children's
Books

a division of Hachette Children's Books

When the first clouds appeared above the hot
African plains, Lazy Lion roared,

"The Big Rain is coming. I will need a roof to
keep me dry. And since I am the King of
the Beasts, I will order a fine house to be built."

So he went to the White Ants.
"Build me a house," he ordered. "A big house!"
The White Ants built a palace of towers
and turrets and chimneys and spires.

But Lazy Lion was too big
to fit through the door.
"I won't live in the earth,"
said Lion crossly.

So he went to the Weaver Birds.
"Build me a house,"
he ordered.
"A big house!"

The Weaver Birds built a nest of grasses and
palm leaves and soft fluffy seeds, and it hung
from the branch of a thorn tree. But Lazy
Lion was too heavy to reach the door.
"I won't live up a tree,"
said Lion crossly.

So he went to
the Ant Bears.
"Build me a house,"
he ordered.
"A big house!"

The Ant Bears dug a huge hole with
many rooms and caverns and tunnels
and caves. But it was damp and so
dark that Lion couldn't see anything.
"I won't live underground," said Lion crossly.

So he went to Honey Badger.
"Build me a house," he ordered. "A big house!"
Honey Badger found a hollow tree stump and
ate all the bees and honeycomb inside it, and
cleaned it as clean as clean, and Lion climbed inside.

But his head stuck out of the hole at the top, and his tail stuck out of the hole at the bottom.

"I won't live in a tree stump," said Lion crossly.

So he went to Crocodile.
"Build me a house," he ordered. "A big house!"

Crocodile found a cave in the river
bank and swept it with his tail, and Lion
walked in and went to sleep. But in the night
the cave filled up with water from the river.
"I won't live in the water," said Lion crossly.

By now Lazy Lion was very,
very cross, and the sky was absolutely
full of big black clouds. So Lion
called all the animals together.
"You must ALL build me a house,"
he ordered. "A VERY, VERY BIG..."

But just as he said the words "VERY, VERY BIG",
there was a flash of lightning in the sky,
and a rumbling of thunder.

Suddenly the Big Rain poured down everywhere.

The Ant Bears rushed underground.
Honey Badger trundled off to his tree stump,
and Crocodile waddled into his cave.

The White Ants marched off down their hole.
The Weaver Birds flapped to their nest.

And they all watched Lion
sitting in the rain in the middle
of the African plain.

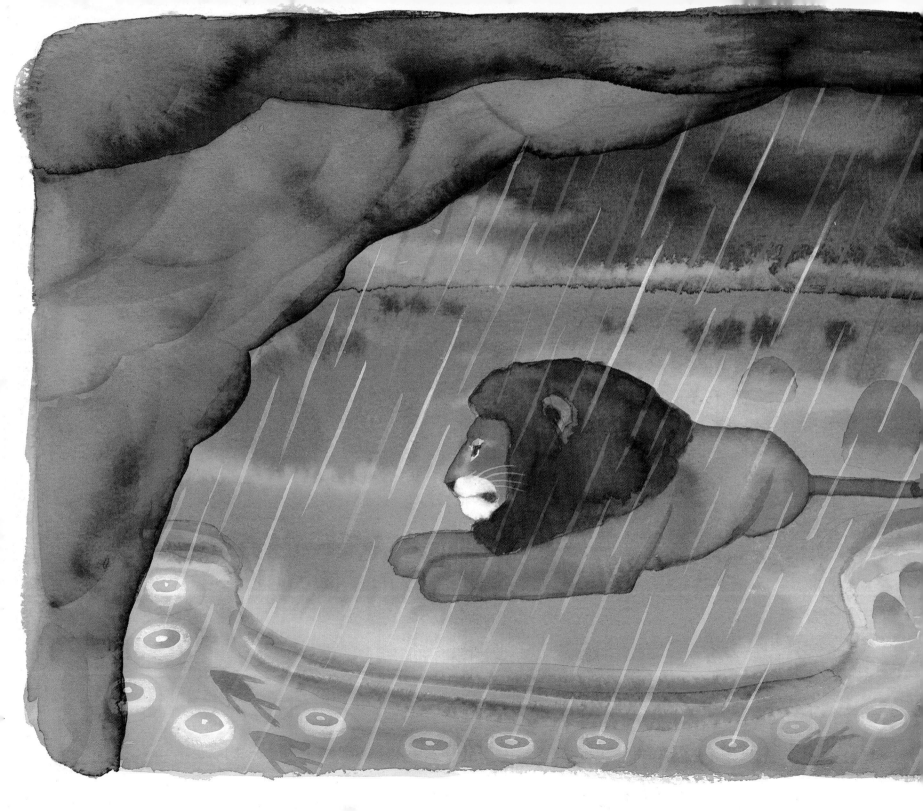

"He is so very difficult to please,"
said Crocodile, snik-snakking his teeth.
And he cried a few tears. Not real ones.
Just little crocodile ones.

And to this day, Lion has not found a house
to live in. So he just wanders the African plain.
On sunny days and cloudy days.
And even in the Big Rains.